This
Treasure Cove Story
belongs to

Alfie Bell

ROCKET TO THE RESCUE!

A CENTUM BOOK 978-1-912396-99-3
Published in Great Britain by Centum Books Ltd.
This edition published 2019.

1 3 5 7 9 10 8 6 4 2

© 2019 MARVEL. All Rights Reserved.

Centum Books Ltd, 20 Devon Square, Newton Abbot,
Devon, TQ12 2HR, UK.

www.centumbooksltd.co.uk | books@centumbooksltd.co.uk
CENTUM BOOKS Limited Reg. No. 07641486.

A CIP catalogue record for this book is available
from the British Library.

Printed in China.

A Treasure Cove Story

MARVEL

GUARDIANS OF THE GALAXY

ROCKET TO THE RESCUE!

By John Sazaklis
Illustrated by Michael Borkowski and Michael Atiyeh

'HEY, YOU!' shouted **ROCKET RACCOON**. 'Come back here with my friend!'

The furry hero chased a cloaked criminal through a crowded marketplace. The thief had snatched **GROOT**, the treelike member of the **GUARDIANS OF THE GALAXY**, who was currently regrowing in a pot.

'Star-Lord! Rev up the ship!' Rocket barked into his communicator. 'The Collector has grabbed Groot!'

THE COLLECTOR was an alien who wanted to own every unique item in the universe. And if he couldn't buy it, he'd *steal* it!

In moments, the Guardians' spaceship, **MILANO**, appeared overhead. Rocket rushed to it, followed by his teammates, **GAMORA** and **DRAX**.

'Sorry to cut the visit to planet Athena short,' Rocket told them. 'But our buddy's been Groot-napped!'

'Don't worry – we'll get him back!' Star-Lord said
as the sleek spaceship streaked out of orbit.

Suddenly, the view screen lit up. It was the Collector!
'Your friend will make a *tree*-rific addition to my
collection,' he laughed. 'I'll take good care of him.'

I am Groot!

Furious, Rocket Raccoon jumped onto the spaceship's control panel.

'We're going too slow!' he shouted, slamming his paw down on the turbo boost button.

The *Milano* hurtled forward at super-speed
– so fast that it zoomed past the Collector's ship!
'Just my luck!' the Collector chuckled. 'Now
I'll blast the Guardians right out of the galaxy!'

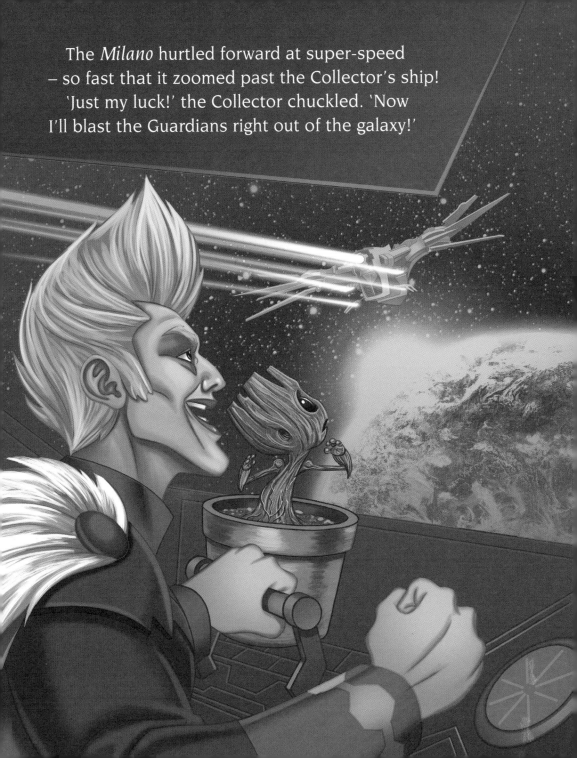

The Collector fired his laser cannons at the *Milano*.

CHOOM!

CHOOM!

Gripping the controls tightly, Star-Lord weaved the spacecraft up and down to avoid the blasts.

'Can you get us back to the Collector's ship?'
Gamora asked.

'I'll get us close enough to knock on his door,'
Star-Lord replied. He turned the *Milano* around
and headed straight for the Collector.

The villain panicked. His ship spiralled out of control

As soon as the Guardians arrived, the heroes raced
to the rescue, with Rocket leading the charge!

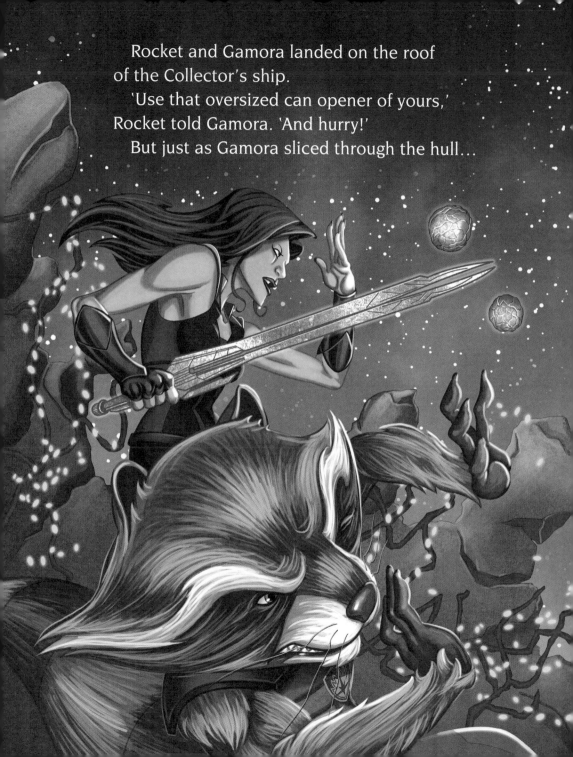

Rocket and Gamora landed on the roof
of the Collector's ship.
'Use that oversized can opener of yours,'
Rocket told Gamora. 'And hurry!'
But just as Gamora sliced through the hull…

... the Collector launched through the hole, wearing a high-tech jet pack. He had Groot in his grip.

'Groot is mine, but you still get a parting gift!' he called out, throwing a handful of glowing pellets. 'Enjoy these **CHITAURI SQUIDPODS**.'

SHOOM!

'Did he say Chitauri Squidpods?'
Star-Lord asked as the pellets hit
the ground.

Large, slimy, tentacle-like vines began to sprout!
'Less talk, more action!' Gamora shouted as she
slashed one of the wildly waving branches.

'Yo, muscleman! I've got an idea. It's time to make the fur fly!' Rocket yelled. Drax flexed his arm and hurled Rocket Raccoon through the air.

'I am Groot!' Groot said when Rocket landed on the Collector's back.

'Unhand me, you vile vermin!' the Collector shrieked.

'I'll give you a hand,' Rocket said, squashing a Squidpod against the Collector's head. 'And a few tentacles, too!'

'*ARGH!* Get it off me!' the Collector cried, dropping Groot.

Rocket dived to catch his friend. 'Don't worry, little buddy. I've got you!' he said.

'And I've got *you*!' Star-Lord said, grabbing them both in midair.

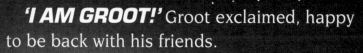

'I AM GROOT!' Groot exclaimed, happy to be back with his friends.

'You're right,' Rocket replied. 'That *was* a great adventure. But what did you expect? **WE'RE THE GUARDIANS OF THE GALAXY!'**

Treasure Cove Stories

Book list may be subject to change.